Favorite Fairy Tales

Gulliver's Travels

Retold by Rochelle Larkin   **Illustrated by Alan Leiner**

CREATIVE CHILD PRESS
is a registered trademark of Playmore Inc.,
Publishers and Waldman Publishing Corp., New York, N.Y.

Once upon a time, a doctor named Lemuel Gulliver was looking for adventure. He took a job on a sailing ship called the *Antelope*, which was headed for the far seas.

All was quiet for the first few months, but then an unexpected storm raged over the ship.

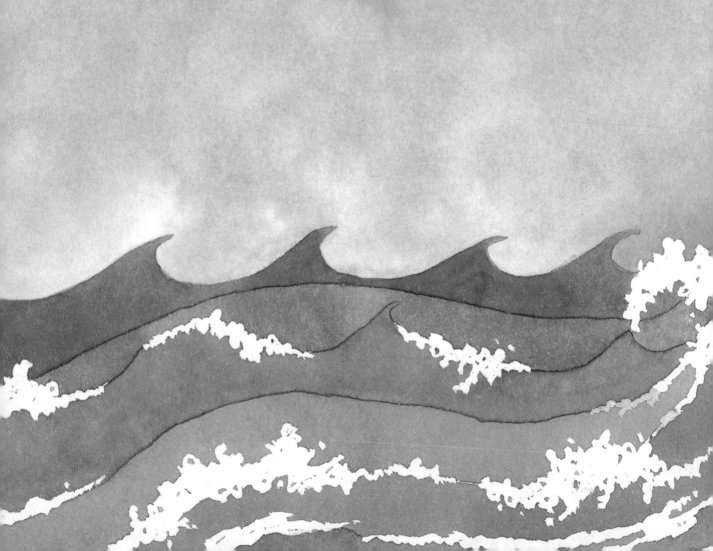

Only Gulliver, keeping afloat on a board, survived.

He washed up on a beach where, exhausted by his ordeal, he fell into a deep sleep.

When he awoke, he found himself tied down by hundreds of tiny ropes, and surrounded by people, perfectly shaped, but only six inches tall!

Gulliver had landed in Lilliput, a kingdom of people and things so small he was a giant in comparison.

It was easy for Gulliver to break out of his bonds, but he was very careful not to hurt any of the tiny Lilliputians. He let them drag him to their capital, where he was brought to the king and queen.

Gulliver reached out and held the king in the palm of his hand.

The brave little king announced: Gulliver would protect Lilliput and its people, and they would provide Gulliver with all his needs.

But feeding someone the size of Gulliver was no easy job for the Lilliputians.

Making him a new suit of clothes was difficult too!

But little by little and by and large, Gulliver and the Lilliputians got used to each other.

Meanwhile, unknown to the Lilliputians, their enemies in the north, the Blefuscudians, were preparing to make war.

They loaded their tiny ships with soldiers and ammunition and set sail from Blefescu to Lilliput.

Soon the sails of their fleet appeared off the coast.

The Lilliputians were totally unprepared. But they had a great secret weapon!

Gulliver! He waded right out into the harbor and pulled all the enemy ships together.

The threat to Lilliput was over. The little people danced in the streets for joy.

Gulliver was the hero of the day. The Lilliputians made him a big medal that said exactly that. Gulliver wore it proudly.

But Gulliver was beginning to feel that he had all the adventures he'd wanted, and more.

He missed his home and his family and thought about them all the time.

Gulliver went to the king and queen to explain how he felt. He loved the Lilliputians, but it was time to go home. The king and queen understood.

All the Lilliputians helped Gulliver build a boat. Then they watched sadly as he sailed away.

And Gulliver told stories about the Lilliputians to his children and grandchildren for many, many happy years afterwards.